Based on the television series *Little Lunch,* produced by Gristmill Pty Ltd. © Screen Australia, Film Victoria and Gristmill Pty Ltd.

"The Snack Shop" is based on the TV episode "The Milk Bar," written by Robyn Butler and Trent Roberts.

"Grandparents Day" is based on the TV episode "The Grandparents Day," written by Robyn Butler and Tim Potter.

"The Cake Sale" is based on the TV episode "The Cake Stall," written by Robyn Butler and Danny Katz.

First U.S. edition 2019

First published by Black Dog Books, an imprint of Walker Books Australia Pty Ltd 2016

Library of Congress Catalog Card Number 2018960078
ISBN 978-0-7636-9471-5

19 20 21 22 23 24 LSC 10 9 8 7 6 5 4 3 2 1

Printed in Crawfordsville, IN, U.S.A.

This book was typeset in New Century Schoolbook and Love Ya Like a Sister. The illustrations were done in ink.

Candlewick Entertainment
an imprint of
Candlewick Press
99 Dover Street
Somerville, Massachusetts 02144

visit us at www.candlewick.com

MIX
Paper from
responsible sources
FSC   FSC® C132124
www.fsc.org

Little Lunch

Triple Treats

Little Lunch

Triple Treats

Danny Katz
illustrated by Mitch Vane

CANDLEWICK
ENTERTAINMENT

BATTIE

gentle

creative

imaginative

ATTICUS

sweet

curious

always hungry

DEBRA-JO

smart

ambitious

organized

MELANIE

determined

courageous

shy

RORY

mischievous

easily distracted

liked by everyone

TAMARA

athletic

energetic

confident

MRS. GONSHA

extremely patient
(with a tendency
to nod off in class)

the SNACK SHOP

Atticus looked in his lunch box.

Yessssss.

Exactly what he wanted for little
lunch: something in a plastic package.
He planned on being an astronaut
one day, and if you want to be an
astronaut, you have to get
used to eating things in
plastic packages.

ATTICUS

PLASTIC

PLASTIC   PLASTIC   PLASTIC

That's pretty much the only training
you need. Being an astronaut is not
as hard as everyone thinks.

Melanie looked in her lunch box.

 **Woooohooooo.**

Exactly what she wanted
for little lunch: no
mandarins. She'd been
getting them all week
and she hated the seeds. She was
a really bad seed-spitter and they
always fell on her shoes, or went
backward down her throat, or just
dribbled down her chin
and hung there like a
little mandarin-seed beard.

2

Battie peeked in his lunch box.

Excellennnnto.

Exactly what he wanted
for little lunch: a stale
sandwich, stale crackers,
and a warm, squishy
cheese stick. Perfect
for building an alien

fortress with sandwich walls, a
cracker roof, and a warm, squishy
solar cheese stick communication
tower.

Rory was about to look in his
lunch box and then—

ohhhhhhhhhh-

he remembered he didn't have a
lunch box. He'd left it at home. Again.

 It was his mom's fault:
every morning she made
his sandwiches, wrapped
his sandwiches, and put
his sandwiches into his
lunch box. Then she left his lunch box
beside his schoolbag on the kitchen
bench for him to put it in. Why
couldn't she put his lunch box in his
schoolbag as well? Why did he have
to do everything? Thanks, Mom.

Thanks a LOT.

Without his lunch box, Rory had
nothing to eat and he was feeling
pretty hungry. He thought of asking
Melanie for some food—she usually
had a spare mandarin to give away—
but he knew she didn't have one

 today just by looking at her.
She didn't have her usual

mandarin-
SEED
BEARD
mandarin-seed beard.

Battie had nothing to give him
either: he'd already turned his little
lunch into an alien fortress. So Rory
couldn't exactly nibble on the cheese
stick communication tower. And
anyway, Battie had covered the whole
fortress with rocks and sand for
camouflage, so even if Rory did

take a nibble, it would be a bit crunchy.

And no way was Atticus going to let Rory anywhere near his lunch box; he even held on to it with both hands while he played foursquare, which is tricky because you need your hands to hit the ball. Atticus had to hit the ball with the front of his head instead.

By now, Rory was feeling pretty tired and a bit weak. He needed something to eat, and fast. Using all his remaining energy,

he shuffled into the school building
and peeked in the lost-and-found

box to see if there
was any old food
that someone had
lost, but there was
just a pair of old
pants—and he wasn't

hungry enough to eat old pants.

He clomped upstairs to the
teachers' lounge to
get an emergency
jam sandwich,
but Mrs. Gonsha
said they'd run out
of jam and bread. He'd
eaten their whole supply

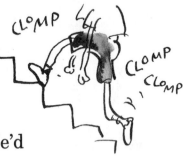

because he'd forgotten his lunch box
every day for the past month.

He dragged his feet downstairs

and made his way to
the hooks where his
schoolbag was hanging.
Maybe, just maybe,
there was an old banana
in there . . . or a granola
bar . . . or a pencil he could suck some
juice out of. He reached inside, felt
around, and right at the bottom he

touched something
hard and smooth
and unfoodlike.
Something that felt
a little bit like . . .

8

Money.

He took it out.

He didn't have
the energy to count
the money, but it
felt exactly like three dollars and
seventy-five cents. A huge, important
question went through his head: If a
person is really, really hungry, and
all they have is three dollars and
seventy-five cents, what can that
person do to stop being really, really
hungry?

He thought . . .

and thought . . .

Then it came to him:

YES,

YES, and

YES.

With a sudden burst of energy,
Rory took off. He ran down the hall,
flew out the school doors, raced across

the playground,
jumped over bushes,
balls, benches, and
Battie (luckily
Battie was bending
over at the time,

picking up a stick to use as an alien

fortress laser-
defense space
cannon).

10

Rory ran all the way to
the school gate and
pressed his face
against the wire
fence so hard he got
crisscross marks on his nose.

He was about to do the unthinkable.
He was ready to do the impossible.
Rory was going to go . . .

Off school grounds.

But before he went anywhere, a voice behind him said, "Rory, what are you looking at?"

He turned around. Debra-Jo was standing there, with everyone else standing beside her: Melanie, Atticus, Tamara, and Battie (holding his laser-defense space-cannon stick). They knew he was up to something. Rory was always up to something.

Rory said, "Uhhhh . . . well . . . I know this is going to sound like just about the worst thing you've ever heard . . . but I'm going to the shop across the road."

Debra-Jo went

"Ohhhhhhhhhhhh,"

because it *was* the worst thing she'd
ever heard. She said, "Rory, you can't
do that! It's against the rules!"

And Tamara said, "Yeah, you'll get
into huuuuge trouble!"

And Battie said, "And you might
never come back! Remember that

13

story about the boy who crossed the road to go to the shop and got picked up by a hawk and they flew away forever to a distant island?" Nobody remembered that  story because Battie was making it up as he went along, but it was still a pretty good story.

Rory said, "Look, I'm hungry, I need food, and I have three dollars and  seventy-five cents to buy something." He showed everyone the money in his hand, and Atticus said, "Actually,

Rory, that's six dollars and eighty cents." And Rory said, "Wow! Even better! That means I can buy all you guys something too!"

Atticus didn't need to think about this for too long: "Great! I'll have fries."

Tamara said, "Yeah, a fruit roll for me."

Melanie said, "I want licorice!"

 And Battie said, "One lollipop, please."

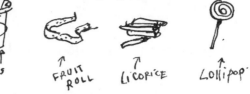

FRIES   FRUIT ROLL   LICORICE   LOLLIPOP

Debra-Jo couldn't believe what she was hearing. It was her job to stop them because she was a student council representative. She was also a school well-being officer and she'd played a police officer in the school play. She turned to Atticus and said, "No one's getting anything from the shop, Atticus! You need to stop Rory! If he walks out that school gate, I'm going to tell on him!"

This was hardly a surprise because Debra-Jo was also the classroom tattletale. She even told on people when there was nothing to tell. One time she told on

Battie for dropping
his pencil in class.
Another time, she
told on Tamara
for doing cartwheels
in the hall.

And there was one time
when she told on Melanie for
not liking broccoli. Even Mrs.
Gonsha thought
that was going
a little too far.

Rory said, "Please Debra-Jo, don't tell on me.

Pleeeeeeeease.

If you don't tell, I'll bring you back a cup of fries."

Debra-Jo thought long and hard about the situation; she didn't really want everyone to be mad at her for ruining Rory's shopping adventure. And she was getting kind of sick of everyone calling her a tattletale all the time. And also, if she was going to be completely honest with herself, she didn't really want to miss out on the

fries. She loved fries: she could almost
smell them coming out of the shop,
drifting across the road, going up
into her nostrils, whispering,

"Debra-Jo . . . don't you want
to eat meeeeeee? I'm Soooo
yummmmmmmmy . . . and
Soooooo salty and hot . . ."

"All right then,
Rory," she said.
"No telling. I promise. I, Debra-Jo, do
solemnly swear that I will not tell—"

But before she could even finish her sentence, Rory had ducked out of the school gate and was heading toward the shop . . .

And at that exact same moment, Mrs. Gonsha stepped out of the school doors and started heading across the playground.

Toward them.

Of course, the first thing Debra-Jo wanted to do was run over to Mrs. Gonsha and tell on Rory, but she'd made a promise, so she tried to control her tattletale brain by chanting in her head,

"Debra, Debra, do not tell."

She turned to her friends. "OK, we need to do something to distract Mrs. Gonsha before she notices Rory is missing. Any ideas?" Tamara had a good idea: maybe they could whip up a quick hip-hop dance number, but was there enough time for the complicated choreography? Battie suggested they could reenact a scene from a movie he saw once about

a robot that was half
human, half monkey
and it lived in a desert—
but nobody was really
listening to him
because nobody knew

what he was talking about.

Mrs. Gonsha was peering around
the playground. She seemed to be
searching for something. There was
no time for any more suggestions.
Debra-Jo said, "Quick! Let's make a
human pyramid! That will distract
her!"

She got everyone to climb on
one another's backs and balance
carefully. It was actually a pretty

good human pyramid for about seven seconds, until Melanie's bony knees started digging into Atticus's unbony back and he fell down, which meant Melanie fell down, which meant everyone fell down.

But it did the job: Mrs. Gonsha stopped looking around, then came over to see what they were doing. She said, "It's good to see you all having so much fun.

"But has anyone seen Rory? He came to the teachers' lounge looking for some food and I've found a few cookies for him."

Of course Debra-Jo really wanted to tell. It was about to come out of her mouth, but she forced the tattle to stay in. Instead, she said, "Uhhh, hey, Mrs. Gonsha, what's the capital of Canberra? I mean Australia! Is it Canberra? Yes! Canberra is the capital of Australia, isn't it? Yes! Canberra! Australia! Australia! Canberra!"

Mrs. Gonsha said, "Debra-Jo, what's going on? Do you know where Rory is?"

Of course Debra-Jo really, *really* needed to tell now. She used all the powers of her brain to hold it back, but it was impossible. The words were coming out. They could not be stopped.

She said, "Uhhh . . . actually . . . he went . . . to the . . . the . . . senior playground, Mrs. Gonsha. Over there. On the other side of the oval."

Mrs. Gonsha said, "Thanks, Debra-Jo," and hurried off to the senior playground. Everyone breathed a sigh of relief. They were very impressed with Debra-Jo for not telling, and Debra-Jo was pretty impressed with herself too, chanting in her head, *Debra, Debra, did not tell.*

Debra, Debra, you did well!

The chanting in her head didn't
last long.

Mrs. Gonsha was
walking toward
them,
holding
Rory by
the shoulder.
And Rory was
getting dragged
along beside her,
holding a sausage roll,
a fruit roll, some licorice, one
lollipop, and two cups of fries.

Mrs. Gonsha looked very angry.
If you were to measure how angry she

was on a scale of one to ten, it would
be at least
forty-seven.
She stopped
in front of the
group and said,

"So who was part of this?"

Everyone put their hand up, except
Battie, who put up his laser-defense
space-cannon stick.

Mrs. Gonsha said, "You are all in

VERY.
BIG.
TROUBLE!

Debra-Jo, I cannot believe you did not
tell me the truth when I asked you
where Rory was."

Debra-Jo said, "I'm sorry Mrs.
Gonsha, but everyone is so sick of
me being a tattletale all the time,
so I stopped myself from doing it."

Mrs. Gonsha said, "This isn't the

same as Melanie
not liking broccoli!
I don't care if Melanie
doesn't like broccoli!

Nobody likes broccoli! But I do care if Rory leaves the school grounds, and I am very, very, very, very, VERY . . ."

Debra-Jo knew what the next word was going to be.

"DISAPPOINTED!!!"

Debra-Jo went

OHHHHH

because this REALLY was the worst thing that she'd ever heard. She wondered what the future would hold for her now. Would she be punished for this? Would her parents be told what happened? Would she lose her student council badge? Would she still be able to be a lawyer when she grew up?

WHAT WAS GOING TO HAPPEN TO POOR DEBRA-JO?????

Mrs. Gonsha gave everyone a big speech about how important it is to always tell the truth, or else terrible things can happen. And after that, Rory had to go to the principal's office and sit in Rory's spot, which is his own special chair facing the wall.

And Melanie, Atticus, Tamara, Battie, and Debra-Jo all had to go and sit in the principal's office as well, on other little chairs beside him.

Rory felt pretty bad that he'd gotten everyone in trouble, but he promised to make it up to them by never *ever* forgetting his lunch box again. But there was still one little problem: he didn't have

his lunch box, and it was almost
lunchtime . . .

He turned around in his chair.
"Uhhhh . . . by the way . . . has
anyone got any spare food?"

GRANDPARENTS DAY

Names for grandparents are always
pretty funny to say out loud.
Debra-Jo called her grandparents
Ooma and Oopa, which sounds
like something you'd hear in the
chorus of a rock song when the
singer has run out of words to sing:
*"Oooomaaaa, ooooopaaaaa,
OOOOOOOMAAAAAAA
YEAHHHHHHH!!!!!"*

OOOMA
OOOPA

Tamara called her grandparents
Po-Po and No-No, which sounds
like two little babies sitting on their
potties, having a conversation. One is
saying "Po-Po?" and the other one is
saying "No-No."

Atticus didn't have a grandfather,
but he called his grandmother Ya-Ya,
which sounds like something a jockey
would yell at her horse in the middle

of a race: "Come on, Fancy Freckles!
Go faster! Let's win this one! YA-
YAAAAAAA!!!!!"

Battie just called his grandfather
Pop. If you say it softly,
it sounds like someone
squeezing a tiny Bubble
Wrap bubble, *poppp*. If you yell
it across a room, it sounds like an

exercise ball
exploding:

37

POPPPPPPPPPPP!!!!!!

Today was Grandparents Day at
school, which is a special day when
all the Oomas and Oopas and Po-Pos
and No-Nos and Ya-Yas and Pops are
invited to the school hall to have tea.
Everyone in class always got really
excited about Grandparents Day
because it meant they got to hang
out with their grandparents and eat
lots of delicious cake. And best of
all, they got the whole morning off
class. That last reason alone made
Grandparents Day one of the best
days of the year.

But Mrs. Gonsha was a bit nervous about Grandparents Day: she wanted to make sure it didn't turn out like last year's Grandparents Day, which was a bit of a disaster.

First of all, the ramp leading up to the school hall had been

closed off because of a termite infestation, so any grandparents who couldn't climb stairs had to stand outside in the pouring rain.

And all the grandparents who managed to get inside the school hall had to listen to Debra-Jo playing John Lennon's "Imagine" on the recorder, which was so bad you had to imagine it was "Imagine." And finally, Rory performed a rap song that he made up all by himself:

"Grandparents: get old and busted
Got no teeth and can only eat custard
uh-huh
Granddads have no hair on their heads
It's in their noses and ears instead,
uh-huh yeah."

And halfway through, a few of the
grandparents stood up and went
outside to stand in the pouring rain
until it was over.

So to make sure this year's
Grandparents Day was extra-
successful and extra-undisastrous,
Mrs. Gonsha had organized
something very special. She'd invited
Battie's grandfather to be the guest of
honor and give a little talk about his
amazing life. Battie's grandfather was

a famous inventor who'd invented
a very important machine that
helped sick people in hospitals. He'd
even won a special award from the
government at a big
important ceremony.
It was a bit like getting
a Student of the Week
certificate, but you had

to wear a suit.

To thank Battie's
grandfather for coming in
to give a speech, Mrs. Gonsha
had spent the last two
weeks knitting him

a lime-green thank-you-for-coming scarf. But Battie was a bit worried. There were two problems with Mrs. Gonsha's lime-green thank-you-for-coming scarf. One problem was that Pop didn't really like the color lime-green very much.

And the second, slightly more massive problem, was . . .

Pop wasn't actually coming to Grandparents Day.

Last night, Pop hadn't felt too well and had gone to the hospital to stay overnight.

He even got to test out the special hospital machine he'd invented and see how it worked up close (because he was actually attached to it). Thankfully, Pop was feeling a lot better now, but he wasn't going to be well enough to come to Grandparents

Day and be the guest of honor.

Battie hadn't told Mrs. Gonsha yet; he was too scared to tell her because he thought she was going to be really disappointed, especially seeing as

she'd gone to so much trouble knitting
that lime-green thank-you-for-coming
scarf. Now she'd have to chuck
the scarf in the trash, or give it to
someone else, or turn it into a lime-
green winter sweater for one of
those really long sausage dogs.

So Battie did the thing that kids
do when they have really bad news
that they're too scared to tell their
teacher.

He went into hiding.

All through
little lunch,
nobody could find
Battie. He hid in
the climbing tree.

He hid in the space
between the buildings.

He hid under a bench.
Then after a while he
thought, *C'mon Battie, this is
ridiculous. You can't hide under a
bench all morning! It's time to be brave*

46

and face up to your responsibilities!
So he crawled out from under the
bench, stood up, and bravely walked

SMELLY DUMPSTER

to a different hiding
spot . . . behind the
old smelly dumpster
near the fence.
From behind the
old smelly dumpster,
Battie had a perfect
view of the front
gate. He could see all the Oomas
and Oopas and Po-Pos and No-Nos
and Ya-Yas starting to arrive for
Grandparents Day. And he could see
Mrs. Gonsha standing at the gate,
greeting them all as they came in,

47

holding the lime-green thank-you-for-coming scarf and looking around for Battie's grandfather.

But there was no Pop popping out of anywhere.

Battie knew that Mrs. Gonsha was going to find out sooner or later— probably when all the grandparents had sat down in the school hall and she introduced Pop but nobody came up to give a speech. There'd be a long, terrible silence, and she'd have to ask Debra-Jo to fill the time by playing "Imagine" on the recorder.

No, no, no. Imagining Debra-Jo playing "Imagine" was too horrible to imagine.

BRRRIIING

That was the school bell. Little lunch was over. Grandparents Day was about to begin and Battie had to do something.

So he did the thing kids do when they need to tell their teacher some really bad news but they're too scared to say it right to their face—he decided to write Mrs. Gonsha a letter. He already had a pencil in his shirt pocket. (Pop taught him to always carry around a pencil in his shirt pocket. And also a sharpener, a protractor, and a small foldable ruler.)

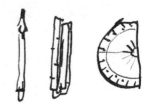

Battie found an old piece of paper
in the dumpster that was pretty clean
on one side. There was a little pink
yogurt blob on the back, but hopefully
Mrs. Gonsha wouldn't see that. Then
he wrote a message to Mrs. Gonsha,
explaining exactly what happened
to Pop and why he couldn't come to
Grandparents Day.

Battie
signed his
name at
the bottom.
Under his
name he
wrote . . .

p.s. Sorry for ruining Grandparents Day. I hope you are not too disappointed.

And under that he wrote . . .

another p.s. Sorry you wasted all that time knitting that lime-green scarf, which looks really nice by the way. You are a good knitter.

And under that he wrote . . .

the last p.s. (I promise): Don't look at the pink yogurt blob on the back of this letter. It's disgusting.

Battie now had to give his letter to Mrs. Gonsha, so he did the thing kids do when they need to give their teacher a letter but they're too scared to go up to the teacher and hand it straight to them. He found an old, empty orange juice bottle in the recycling, popped the letter inside the bottle, then screwed the lid of the bottle back on tight.

He snuck out from behind the trash cans and crawled to a nearby drain.

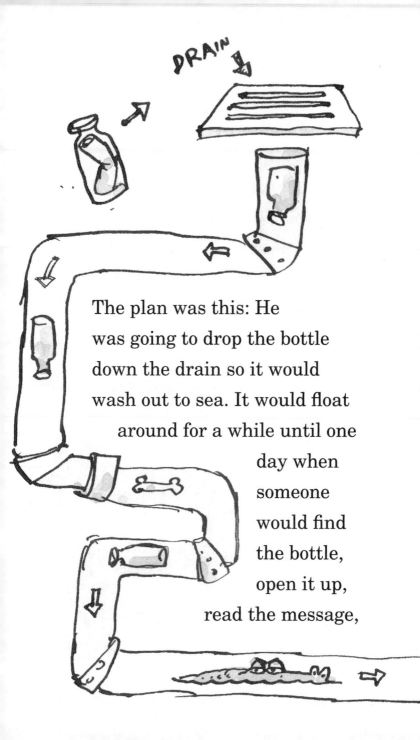

DRAIN

The plan was this: He
was going to drop the bottle
down the drain so it would
wash out to sea. It would float
around for a while until one
day when
someone
would find
the bottle,
open it up,
read the message,

look up Mrs. Gonsha's address on the Internet, then send it to her in the mail. Then she would get Battie's letter and read it and find out why Pop couldn't come to Grandparents Day.

Yep, it was a pretty clever plan. According to Battie's calculations, she should get the letter in twelve years if the ocean currents were fast and the winds were strong, and the person who found the bottle knew how to read English, and the letter hadn't gotten too wet from—

"BATTIE!!"

Twelve years turned out to be twelve seconds.

Mrs. Gonsha was standing over him, holding the lime-green thank-you-for-coming scarf.

She said,

"Were you about to drop that bottle into that drain? You know that's wrong! That bottle will end up as pollution in the ocean!"

Battie said nothing, just held on to the bottle.

Mrs. Gonsha said,

"Battie, is that a piece of paper in the bottle?"

Battie said nothing, just held on to the bottle.

Mrs. Gonsha said,

"Battie, is there something written on that piece of paper?"

Battie said nothing, just handed the bottle to her.

Mrs. Gonsha opened the bottle, took out the letter, and read it. Battie watched her face to see if she looked disappointed, but she didn't look disappointed at all. She just nodded and sighed a bit. When she finished reading the letter, she bent down and gave him a hug. She told him she was really sorry Pop wasn't feeling well and that Grandparents Day wasn't ruined at all. She also said she would send the lime-green thank-you-for-coming scarf to the hospital and Pop could use it as a lime-green hope-you-get-better blanket instead.

Battie was pretty happy that Mrs.
Gonsha wouldn't have to throw the

scarf away, or turn it

into a winter sweater

for a sausage dog.

That sounded like a
lot of hard work.

Just then, he noticed a red flashing
light behind him. The kind of red
flashing light you see on the top of
police cars and fire engines and
also . . . ambulances.

Parked just
outside the
school gate
was an
ambulance

with its back door open. Two big
ambulance guys were carrying
out someone in a
wheelchair. Someone

FOLDABLE RULER
with gray hair, a funny
beard, and . . . a small
foldable ruler poking
out of his shirt pocket.
Battie couldn't
believe it. He ran over and gave
Pop a hug. Pop explained that he
wouldn't have missed Grandparents
Day for anything. And because he
had invented such a famous hospital
machine, the nurses and doctors did
him a huge favor and organized an
ambulance to bring him here.

So Grandparents Day went ahead as planned. Battie pushed Pop's wheelchair into the school hall—luckily there was no termite infestation in the ramp this year—and Pop joined all the Oomas and Oopas and Po-Pos and No-Nos and Ya-Yas. Then when it was time for the guest of honor to give his speech, Pop wasn't feeling well enough to stand up and talk, so Battie stood up and talked instead. He told everyone that he loved Pop more than anyone in the whole world. That Pop was a great inventor, but he didn't just invent a famous hospital machine— he invented lots of other stuff too,

fun stuff, and Battie had helped him.
They once made a musical marble-
rolling instrument where you rolled
a marble down a long tube and it hit
lots of different-size glass bottles so it
played a little tune.

Another time they made a massive
fake volcano that squirted foamy lava

all over the backyard and they had to clean it off the lawn and the fence . . .

and the neighbor's roof.

And they even made a stretchy rubber arm so that Battie could pretend he was a superhero named Stretcho. The rubber arm was so stretchy that when he gave him a hug, he could reach around him three and three-quarter times.

STRETCHO ARM

Battie's speech was so entertaining and funny and perfect that all the Oomas and Oopas and Po-Pos and No-Nos and Ya-Yas and Pops clapped and cheered at the end of it. And they kept clapping and cheering for so long that there was no time left for Debra-Jo to play "Imagine" on the recorder.

Was it the best Grandparents Day ever?

THE CAKE SALE

The cake was brown.

The cake was lumpy.

The cake had a fly buzzing around it. Then the fly buzzed away, because the cake was too disgusting even for a fly to go near.

I'M OUT OF HERE

The cake was for sale. Melanie had baked it herself last night and brought it to school for a very special reason. She was going to sell slices of cake to raise money for homeless puppies, because she loved puppies and she hated the thought of a puppy that didn't have a home.

So at the start of little lunch she asked Tamara and Debra-Jo to help her set up a cake sale. They carried a table out into the playground, Melanie put her cake on top of the table, then she started yelling at everyone who walked past,

And lots of kids came over to the table because everyone wants to help homeless puppies. But as soon as they saw the cake, they backed away fast. It was a weird shape and a weird color and it smelled a bit weird too, almost like a homeless puppy.

Tamara and Debra-Jo stood behind the table with Melanie, both of them staring at the cake, not wanting to get too close.

They knew exactly why no one was buying a slice, but they weren't going to say anything to Melanie in case it hurt her feelings.

This cake was not good.

It was supposed to be a ginger hedgehog cake but the school had strict food rules so Melanie wasn't allowed to use any gluten, nuts, milk, or shellfish (which was fine, because the recipe didn't have shellfish in it).

Worse than that, the ginger hedgehog cake was also made with no sugar, no flour, no salt, and no ginger, because Melanie didn't like ginger.

And even WORSE than that, the ginger hedgehog cake had no eggs, no butter, no flavor, no texture and . . . no customers.

Rory, Atticus, and Battie came over to the table, but they didn't come over to buy cake. They came over to make fun of the cake. Rory pointed at it and said,

"Ha-ha, Melanie, too bad nobody's

buying your disgusting ginger hedgehog cake!"

and Melanie said,

"It's not disgusting!"

Atticus looked closely at the cake and said, "Hey, Melanie, maybe you would've had more luck if you made a ginger puppy cake and raised money for homeless hedgehogs!"

Melanie said,

Awwww

"That's not even funny, Atticus!"

Rory looked even closer at the cake and said, "Actually, I think you did make it with puppies. Look! I can see a puppy snout poking out!"

Melanie said,

WOOF WOOF

"That's not a puppy snout! It's just a bit of chocolate that didn't melt!"

Although to be honest, Melanie wasn't sure what was poking out of her cake—she hadn't actually put any chocolate in it.

The boys were being pretty mean, so Melanie decided to just ignore them and go back to her important fund-raising job. She spotted Mrs. Gonsha walking past, so she yelled, "Hey, Mrs. Gonsha! Would you like to help puppies who don't have a home?"

Mrs. Gonsha said, "Of course," and she came over to the table, looking very impressed. She said, "I'm so proud of you girls, giving up your little lunch to raise money for such an excellent cause. You have shown great initiative and I am going to make sure you all collect a Principal's Award for this!"

Melanie said, "Thanks, Mrs. Gonsha. So will you buy a slice of cake then?"

Mrs. Gonsha looked at the cake, took a little sniff, went a bit pale, and said, "Uhhhh . . . yessss. . . . I just have to get my wallet . . . which I left . . . uhhhhh . . . somewhere . . . in . . . some place." She took off across the playground fast. Melanie felt very pleased because her teacher was in such a big hurry to get her wallet.

But Atticus wasn't too pleased about it. It wasn't fair that the girls were going to get Principal's Awards for making

a terrible cake that no one wanted
to buy. And he really wanted to get a
Principal's Award, too. Even Rory had
one. It didn't matter that he stole it
from the principal's desk when he was
in trouble in the principal's office.

Atticus dragged Rory and Battie
away from the table and led them
around the corner, where they had
a boy conference. Atticus said, "We
should start a fund-raiser so we can
win our own Principal's Awards!"

Battie said, "Great idea,
Atticus! We can raise
money for homeless
kittens. They're cuter
than homeless puppies!"

AWWW

Rory said, "Nah, we need something better than puppies and kittens! We need something really serious! Wasn't there an earthquake nearby?"

Atticus said, "Uhhhh, I don't think so."

Rory said, "How about we raise money for my Auntie Becky? Someone stole her lawnmower. Now she can't mow her lawn. It's really serious. The grass is getting high!"

Atticus said, "Uhhhh, I don't think so."

AUNTIE BECKY

With that, the boys were out of ideas. They couldn't think of anything else. That was the end of their fund-raising plan.

Until Battie spoke up. "Hey, I have an idea. My dad has diabetes. We could raise money for diabetes awareness and medical research."

Rory wasn't sure what diabetes was. He said, "Isn't that where you can't stop going to the bathroom?"

"No, that's diarrhea. Diabetes is where you have high blood sugar levels so you have to be careful of what you eat because—"

Rory interrupted,

"Because you can't stop going to the bathroom! That's what I said."

Atticus liked what he was hearing. "Look, it doesn't matter what diabetes is. The point is, diabetes has the word *die* in it. DIE-a-betes. That sounds pretty serious,

so it's the perfect cause for us! Come on, let's raise money for

DIE-A-BETES"

The boys needed a table, so they found an empty trash can, tipped it upside down, then plonked it directly opposite the girls' cake sale. They put their lunch boxes on top of the upside-down can

and started selling whatever food
they had. Atticus had a super salami
sandwich,

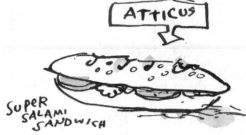

Battie had a
box of raisins,

and Rory had
nothing because he'd forgotten his
lunch box.

Again.

Atticus started yelling,

"HELP BRING AN
END TO DIE-A-BETES!
ONE DOLLAR
FOR A SLICE
OF SUPER
SALAMI
SANDWICH."

And Rory was yelling,

"FIVE CENTS FOR A
RAISIN. TEN CENTS
FOR THREE
RAISINS."

5¢

10¢

"HELP BATTIE'S DAD BECAUSE HE CAN'T STOP GOING TO THE BATHROOM!"

FOR DIE-A-BETES

And Battie just stood there, not saying anything, wishing he'd never suggested diabetes in the first place.

Of course Melanie, Tamara, and Debra-Jo were not too thrilled about the boys setting up a fund-raiser table directly opposite their own fund-raiser table. It was hard enough trying to sell a single piece of ginger hedgehog cake, and things were going to get even harder now that they had competition. On top of that, Atticus's sandwich did look pretty delicious, with salami and cheese and bread and gluten and dairy and seeds—all the stuff that the school didn't allow, but all the stuff that people actually liked to eat. So Tamara decided to fix the problem. She snuck over to the boys' stall, grabbed the super salami sandwich, and ran off with it.

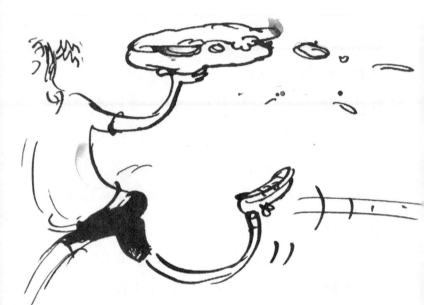

She was the fastest kid in school,
so Atticus couldn't catch her, and
neither could Rory. Battie didn't even
bother—he was a very slow runner,
so he just sat on a bench and watched.

Atticus and Rory chased Tamara all the way to the far end of the playground. Then they chased her all the way back to the cake sale. But they were never going to catch her, so they gave up and just stood there exhausted while she danced around in front of them, waving the sandwich in the air and yelling,

"WHO WANTS TO HELP HOMELESS PUPPIES? ONE DOLLAR A SLICE OF SUPER SALAMI SANDWICH."

YAY

Atticus wasn't
going to let the girls
get away with this.
He stepped up to their
table and said, "OK, if you girls are
going to steal our sandwich, we're
going to steal your cake!" He picked
up the whole ginger hedgehog cake
and threw it over to Battie, yelling,

"HEY, BATTIE.
CATCH!"

But Battie was not only a very slow runner, he was also a very slow catcher, so he didn't catch the ginger hedgehog cake with his hands. He caught the ginger hedgehog cake with the top of his head. It splattered all over his face, but he didn't mind too much. He quite liked the cake—

it wasn't too sweet, and it had a nice brown lumpy taste.

Tamara yelled at Atticus,

" HEY, YOU
WRECKED OUR CAKE!"

and Atticus yelled back,

"YEAH, WELL,
YOU STOLE OUR
SANDWICH!"

and Tamara yelled back,
"OK THEN, HOW
ABOUT I GIVE YOUR

SANDWICH BACK?"
and she tore a big

chunk off Atticus's

90

super salami sandwich and threw it
at him, but Atticus ducked and it hit
Battie right in the face. Battie didn't
mind too much. He quite liked the taste
of the sandwich,
too—it went
very well
with the cake.

Tensions were high, faces
were fierce, something
was about to happen . . .

a food fight.

Atticus grabbed
a blob of cake
off Battie's head
and threw it at
Tamara, but she
ducked and it hit Debra-Jo. Debra-Jo
grabbed a chunk of sandwich from
Battie's face and threw it at Atticus,
but he ducked and it hit Rory. Rory
chucked sandwich, Debra-Jo chucked
cake, Atticus chucked sandwich,
Tamara chucked cake. And while all

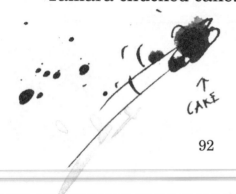

this was going
on, Melanie
went over to

92

Battie, sat down next to him on the bench, and said, "I'm sorry you got cake all over your head."

CAKE

And he said, "That's all right, it's kind of yummy, actually."

Melanie said, "And I'm sorry about your dad's diabetes."

And he said, "Yeah, and I'm sorry about the homeless puppies."

Then they just sat quietly together and watched the food fight.

BEET

Blobs of cake and chunks of sandwich got chucked back and forth, back and forth. Then there was the exact moment when a blob of cake and a chunk of sandwich got chucked in exactly the same direction at exactly the same time, exactly when Mrs. Gonsha was stepping around the corner.

Slowly Mrs. Gonsha peeled a bit of salami off her forehead, flicked a lump of cake from her cheek, and wiped a glob of cheese off her mouth. Only then could you make out the expression on her face.

It was not a particularly happy one. She said,

"WHAT IS GOING ON HERE?"

as a blob of cake fell off her ear.

Debra-Jo said, "It's the boys' fault! We just wanted to do something nice for the homeless puppies and they ruined everything!"

And Atticus said, "No, it's the girls' fault! We just wanted to do something even nicer for Battie's dad and they ruined everything!"

Mrs. Gonsha said, "Are you honestly telling me that all this fighting and yelling and throwing food has something to do with fund-raising?"

None of the girls or the boys could answer that, because they honestly didn't know.

Mrs. Gonsha said, "All of you will

clean this mess up immediately, and
then you will sit in the classroom
at lunchtime and think about the
importance of respecting food and one
another!"

So the six of them had to clean up
the mess, then clean up themselves,
then go to the lost-and-found box to
find clean clothes to wear for the rest
of the day. Battie
had to wear
a tennis skirt
because it was
all that was left.

And at lunchtime,
the six of them had
to sit in the

classroom and think about the important lesson they'd learned that morning. Nobody made any money for puppies, nobody raised any dollars for diabetes, and nobody got a Principal's Award. Although Rory did make one for himself using notebook paper, colored markers, and some gold glitter foil he found in the classroom craft box.

Danny Katz is an author and a newspaper columnist for the *Sydney Morning Herald* who is famous for his larger-than-life characters. He is the author of a number of books for children, including the Little Lunch series. Danny Katz lives in Melbourne, Australia.

Mitch Vane is the illustrator of many children's books and has also worked on storyboards, posters, package design, coloring books, cartoons, editorial illustrations, and paintings. She lives in Melbourne, Australia.